THANK YOU, MISS DOOVER

BY *Robin Pulver*

ILLUSTRATED BY
Stephanie Roth Sisson

Holiday House / New York

For my great (in more ways than one) nephews:
Noah, Ben, T.J., and Dylan. With many versions of
thanks to Mary Cash, my very own Miss Doover.
—R. P.

For my son, Tristam
—S. R. S.

www.holidayhouse.com
First Edition
1 3 5 7 9 10 8 6 4 2

Library of Congress Cataloging-in-Publication Data
Pulver, Robin.
Thank you, Miss Doover / by Robin Pulver ; illustrated by Stephanie Roth Sisson. – 1st ed.
p. cm.
Summary: Jack learns the value of revision as he practices Miss Doover's lesson on
how to write a proper thank-you note.
ISBN 978-0-8234-2046-9 (hardcover)
[1. Thank-you notes–Fiction. 2. Schools–Fiction. 3. Humorous stories.]
I. Sisson, Stephanie Roth, ill. II. Title.
PZ7.P97325Th 2010   2009029949
[E]–dc22

Dear Great-Aunt Gertie,
Thank you for the present!
Love,
Jack
Done!

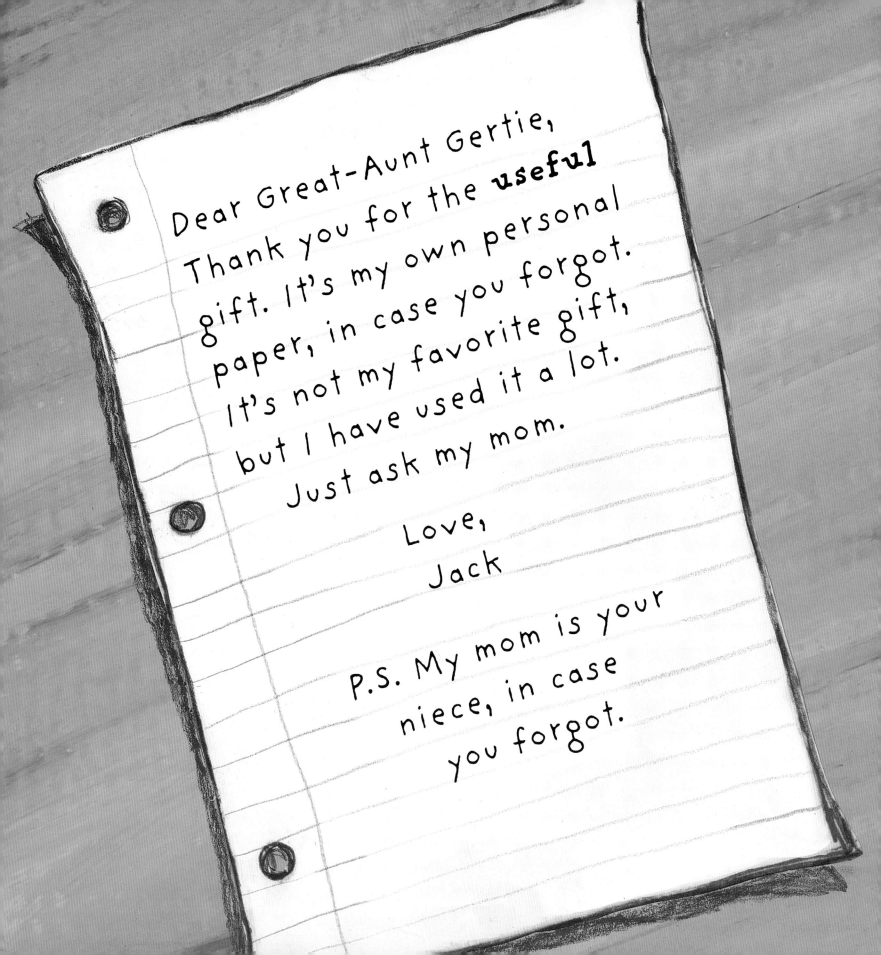

Dear Great-Aunt Gertie,

Thank you for the useful paper. Mom calls it stashunaree, but I don't think it needs a name, because it already has MY name on every piece. That's how Mr. Wilson figured out where the wadded-up paper balls and paper airplanes in his yard came from.

Love,
Jack

P.S. Fetching isn't Puddly's best trick.

Express
Express means to put your thoughts into words.
What's express?
Accomplish means to successfully finish or complete.
Accomplish

Dear Great-Aunt Gertie,
Thank you for the stationery
with my name on it. It will
always remind me of you
because it is GREAT. Your
gift was useful for the whole
family, especially when
Mom asked me to put
down papers fast.
He can't talk with words,
but Puddly chose your gift as
the place of honor to express
his thanks. Puddly made
mistakes in other places before
he accomplished his goal.
Love,
Jack

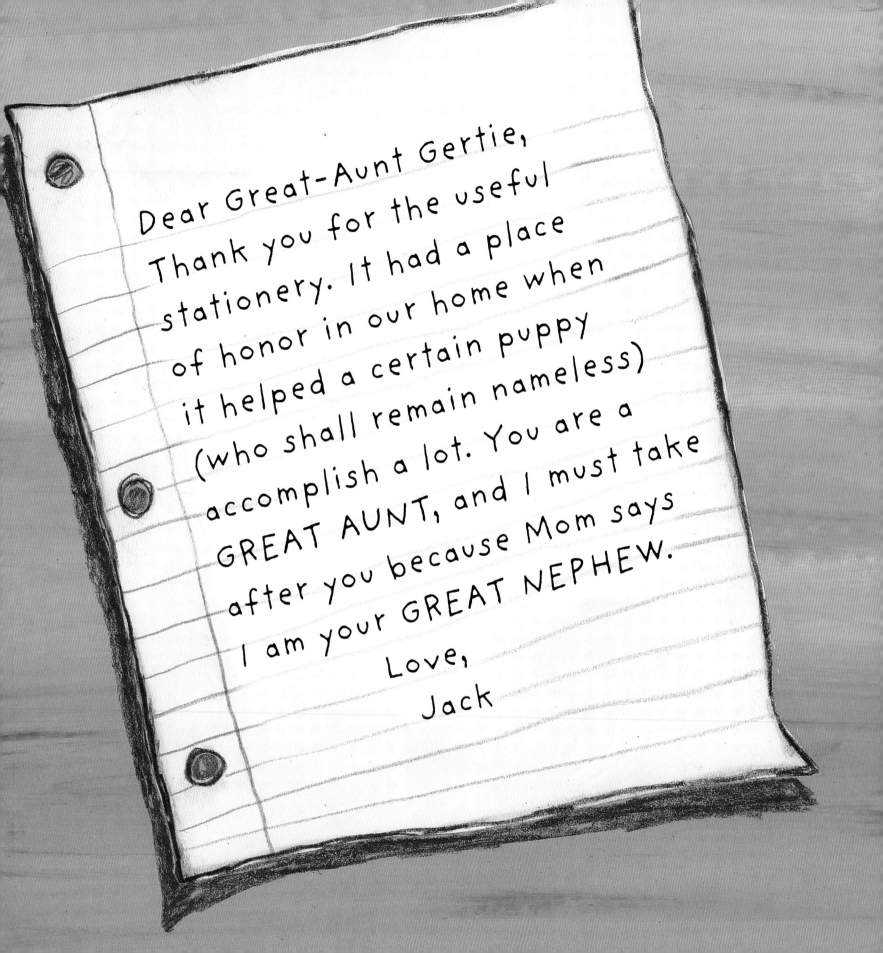

Dear Great-Aunt Gertie,
Thank you for the useful
stationery. It had a place
of honor in our home when
it helped a certain puppy
(who shall remain nameless)
accomplish a lot. You are a
GREAT AUNT, and I must take
after you because Mom says
I am your GREAT NEPHEW.
Love,
Jack

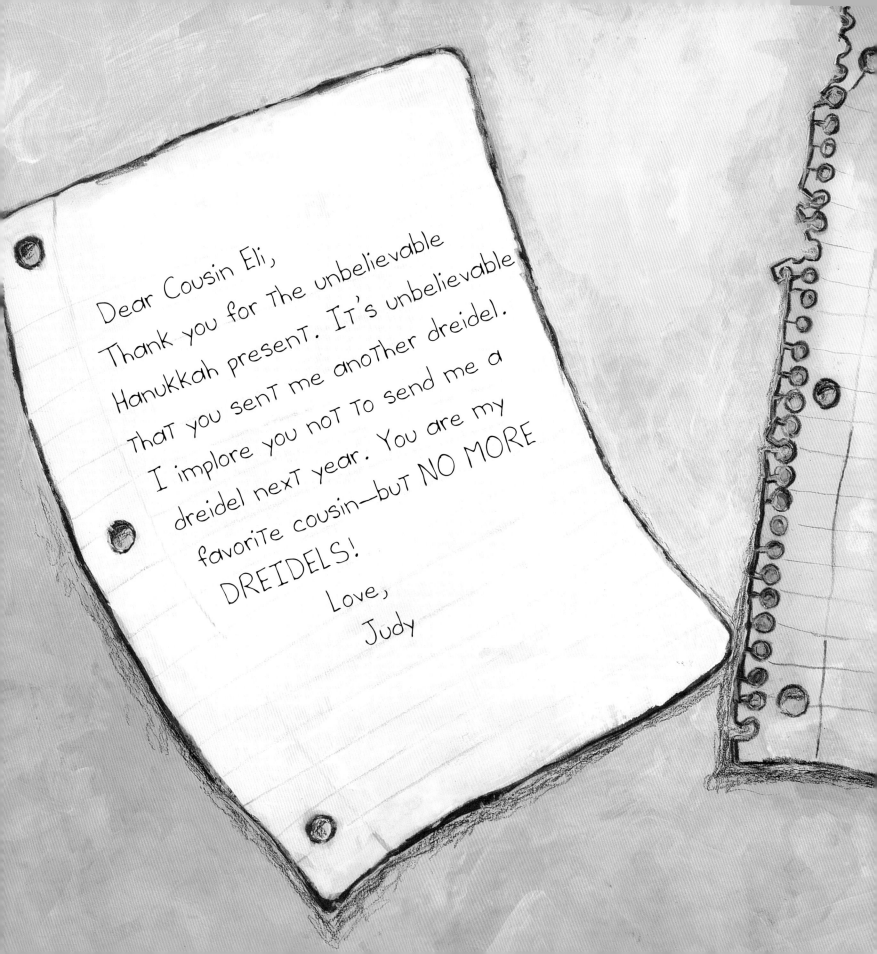

Dear Uncle Joe,
Thank you for the magic kit. I regret that it did not make my brother disappear. I can't express how much I hope you will send a better magic kit next year so that I can accomplish my goal.

Dad says you were a bratty brother, but I bet you were nicer than Tommy.

Love,
Dot

Dear Grandma,
Thank you for the terrific baseball bat. It will always remind me of you. That's because on my favorite TV show, everybody calls the grandma the Old Bat.

Love,
PJ

Dear Miss Doover,
Thank you for making me do things over and over again. You don't give up on me. You will always have a place of honor in my classroom. I regret that you won't be my teacher next year because I am your best student.
Maybe you are related to me and Great-Aunt Gertie because you are a GREAT TEACHER!
Love,
Jack
P.S. Hey! I figured out why your name is Miss Doover!